Table of Conte

CW01500196

FOREWORD

If you are searching for suspenseful, heart-wrenching adventures and tales of teenagers surviving in the world of the undead, these mini sagas are for you.

I've been a fan of zombie movies and stories for as long as I can remember. However, they are retelling the same story of zombies: Adults trying to survive them and their attacks. I've always wondered what it would be like if teenagers had to deal with a zombie apocalypse. . . on their own. How would they handle this outbreak without their parents and other adults? What decisions can they make to ensure their survival? What fate lies ahead of them? Do they survive or become zombies themselves?

Having these ideas in my mind, I've decided to come up with these stories about teenagers in various cities worldwide dealing with zombies on their own and what choices they face to survive. That sounded easy, but the challenge was to keep them as grounded in reality as much as possible given that people haven't dealt with a zombie outbreak . . . yet.

So, enter a world where a zombie apocalypse has taken over the world and left humanity doing what they need to survive, but from the perspective of teens as the central characters.

Enjoy!

Andrew Davidson

Chapter 1: Maya- New York City

"Seriously! WTF?!" thought 17-year-old Maya as she headed toward her hidden sanctuary above her favorite pizzeria. Outside on the desolate Manhattan streets was crawling with nothing but the undead. Surviving on her own in this urban graveyard for the past few months has taught her the importance of being silent, safe, and most importantly . . . a survivor.

"Damn Deadheads. What brought them here?" she asked herself as she grabbed the hunting knife her dad had given her before. . . before all of this. The memories of what happened that day still haunt her dreams. She knows that noise means unwanted attention and a year ago, Manhattan was a noisy place.

As she prepared to leave, she noticed something peculiar in one of the abandoned cars. It appeared to be a boy no more than 12 years old with a scared look on his face. She knew she had to do something. But what? If she helps him, can she trust him? If she doesn't, can she go on knowing she could've saved another survivor?

She made her decision.

Looking inside of her backpack, she pulled out the fireworks and matches she found near the Flatiron Building. She then lit the fireworks making them go off and distracting those cursed Deadheads. Slowly the undead snarled and walked towards the fireworks hoping to satisfy their hunger for human flesh. Maya then raced to the car, opened the door, and told the boy to run with her. They then navigated the streets and alleys avoiding Deadheads and their rotting bodies.

It wasn't until they ran inside of an abandoned bookstore that they caught their breath and introduced themselves.

"Thanks. I'm Alex." He said in between deep breaths.

"Maya", she responded. "What the hell were you thinking back there?"

"I was hungry and was looking for food. I haven't eaten anything in 2 days and thought there would be something in that pizzeria." Alex's stomach started to growl fiercely as he started talking about food. Maya heard it loud and clear and offered him a bag of beef jerky past its expiration date, but it was still better than eating nothing.

Alex began wolfing down the bag of dried, salty meat that had little to no flavor when Maya asked what happened to him. "My family and I used to live in the Upper West Side when *it* happened. My mom was a doctor and tried to help as many people as possible. My dad was told to come to DC for some medical thing since he's a doctor too with the Navy. He told us he had something important to work on and if anything happens to come down to DC. After that, we didn't hear from him again. Phones and internet went down and everyone went into panic mode. My mom and I had to leave our home as the people she was helping turned into those things and started attacking others." Alex then started to cry when he mentioned his mother.

Maya noticed the tears Alex was trying to fight back that found their way falling down his face. She then grabbed his hands offering support. Alex then continued his story. "My mother and I found shelter in places like hospitals and police stations. She was still helping people only a few days until. . ." His voice tapered off.

"She was bit," Maya whispered. Alex nodded his head while a stream of tears fell from his eyes. Maya then wrapped her arms around Alex letting him cry on her. Several minutes went by when Alex started to calm down. Maya wanted to cry as well, but she kept her emotions in check as she knew that if she became emotional, she wouldn't be strong. She thought of the last time she cried. Just a year ago, after "The Outbreak". That's when those Deadheads found the camp, she was a member of on the Brooklyn Bridge and began their feast. Most of the living fought back with guns or whatever they had. Others held onto their loved ones thinking this was their last days living. Maya was one of the few who took their chance jumping into the East River. Upon hitting the bone-chilling water, Maya passed out. She then found herself huddled atop a sunken ship in the water near Pier 11. For the first time since she lost her father, she found herself alone and cried. Until she rescued Alex.

"Looks like we better get going Alex," Maya mentioned.

"Where we going Maya?" Alex responded wiping the dried tears from his face.

"I don't know," Maya paused. "But I'm guessing that Washington DC must be nice this time of the year."

Jack then smiled with a glimmer of hope in his eyes.

Chapter 2: Cynthia & Jack - Los Angeles

L.A. isn't the City of Angels anymore. It's now the City of the Dead. At least that's what Cynthia and Jake believe. The two 16-year-olds found themselves alone in a world gone to ruin after "The Incident". Cynthia knew the city thanks to her father being a bus driver while Jack knew survival skills thanks to his Army Ranger father.

"Sooooo Jackie Boy, where we going tonight?" asked Cynthia.

At first, he hated that name, but since the two shared a passionate kiss that one night and expressed how they felt about each other, he let it go. "I don't know babe. But we're gonna need some medical supplies and ammo." Jack responded while holding his shotgun. Cynthia smiled at her boo noticing how his confidence grew after that night. She never had a boyfriend before, especially a serious one, and vowed that even if the world went to hell, she'd defend Jack with her last breath, and he'd do the same to defend hers.

The two love-struck orphans started to walk into a tunnel that fed the L.A. River, where it started to get darker with every step. Cynthia turned her flashlight on when Jack noticed some movement in the distance. Raising his shotgun, he told Cynthia to get behind him. To their surprise, it was only a cat chasing a rat. Laughing to ease the tension, they quickly stopped when they heard "it".

"Shhhhhh. They'll hear you". Cynthia's face turned pale as a ghost while Jack's heartbeat was racing like his dad's old Corvette when "it" appeared.

Jack aimed his shotgun in hand only to find that "It" was an old man with gray hair and beard wearing old, tattered clothes, walking with a slight limp as if he hurt his leg.

"Name's Pete. Why you in my home?" he inquired angrily with a semi-toothless snarl.

"We were looking for supplies and thought we could take a shortcut through this tunnel." Jack calmly responded.

"Well, you ain't gonna find nothing here 'cept darkness and rats. So Get!!" Pete shouted at the couple. But Cynthia didn't want to go back out into the open and knew this tunnel led to her home in Glendale and asked if they could go on.

"NO! Last time folks came through, they tried to attack me and one of 'em even bit me. Beat the crap out of 'em and left 'em to rot down there. That's what those bastards get." Pete shouted.

"Why would people bite?" pondered Cynthia to herself. "Sorry to hear that, but we *REALLY* need to go this way. Can we at least stay the night without walking into those things?"

Pete looked at the couple and told them they could stay, as long as they stayed near the opening and leave him be. He then hobbled away with a noticeable bite mark on his left calf that looked to be fresh as it was still pouring blood out of the wound. He then disappeared into the darkness of the tunnel. After 15 minutes of settling in, Cynthia then broke the silence between her and Jack.

"Sooooo. . . did you notice the bite on his calf Jackie Boy? What's up with that?", she questioned.

"I don't know babe. Something seems a little off though." Jack held her and looked into her brown eyes with his blue and green eyes reassuring her that he'd keep her safe. He then brushed the hair away from her face and kissed her passionately. She returned the kiss with the same intensity and passion. Only a few minutes later, they heard a growling sound coming from the darkness. Thinking it was a cat, they ignored it. That is until it became louder deep inside the tunnel the two lovers got up ready to fight if needed.

Hobbling toward them was Pete, but something was different about him. His skin was pale. His guttural snarling and remaining teeth were noticeable. And his eyes. . . Jack remembered seeing those eyes on those things that attacked his family.

"GET BEHIND ME!!" Jack yelled to Cynthia. He then grabbed his shotgun and fired a round into Pete's chest, but he was still hobbling. Knowing he had one round left, Jack aimed for Pete's head. BLAM!!! The shot rang out taking Pete's head clean off. Cynthia, shaken with fear, was calmed down by Jack. "We gotta leave Cyn. NOW!!"

They hurried, grabbing whatever they could find, and packed it up. That's when they heard more snarling and saw more of those things walking toward them with hunger in their eyes. The young couple escaped into the open river and ran as fast as they could toward the other side. Once they climbed themselves on the street, they realized that they were once again in the desolate and dark city, alone and in the open, with those things lurking around.

"Come on Cyn. We gotta find someplace safe for the night." Jack mentioned. Cynthia nodded silently, still shaken up by that encounter. After exploring the area for about a few miles, they saw what appeared to be a motel. After opening the door to one of the rooms, Jack inspected it clearly, making sure nobody nor one of those things was inside. He gave Cynthia the "all clear" sign and she then came in. They then barricaded the door and window to ensure that they'd be safe with what was available in the room, including the bed, headboard, and frame. They then settled in for the night holding onto each other.

When the sun rose, Jack and Cynthia woke up with stiff and sore muscles having slept on the unforgiving floor. Gathering their belongings and planning to get supplies, the couple was ready to set out and tackle a new day. Together as usual.

It came as a surprise when they heard a thunderous knock on the door and a deep booming voice telling them to come on out.

Chapter 3: Skylar- Paris

In the dark streets of Paris, the once-known City of Lights dimmed forever. It had been two months after the outbreak and countless Parisians fell victim one way or another. Sixteen-year-old Skylar darted between abandoned cars, her heart pounding in rhythm with her frantic footsteps. The once bustling city now lay silent, its eerie stillness broken only by distant moans of the undead. She had lost her group days ago, leaving her to navigate the now City of Dead alone.

As dusk settled, a desperate whimper echoed through an alley. Cautiously, Skylar followed the sound to find a small, trembling dog huddled behind a dumpster. Its eyes held a haunted intelligence, a survivor like her. She hesitated, torn between her survival and compassion for the vulnerable creature.

With trembling hands, she extended them, offering the dog what little comfort she could. As she scooped it into her arms, she felt a flicker of hope amidst the chaos—a fragile bond in a world turned upside down. She held onto the dog content knowing that she wasn't alone. She had a companion. Together, they ventured into the unknown, two souls clinging to each other in the face of relentless terror.

Skylar named the dog Fleur after its golden-brown coat. She figured Fleur was a young Belgian Malinois having seen them being trained by her father's police department in her younger and innocent days. Skylar knew that these dogs loved being active, possessed a ferocious bite, obeyed commands, and above all, were loyal to their partner. Skylar remembered the training and attempted to recreate it. A daunting task to most people, but Skylar saw herself as a determined young woman who labored for her results.

Several months passed, and thanks to her training, Fleur has been a vital partner in keeping both survivors alive. Fleur was able to find food for them, secure possible places to spend the night, and above all, alert Skylar of the presence of those ravenous undead beings. They had a system in which Fleur would bark to get their attention while Skylar would drive her makeshift spear forged from a piece of rebar into their head ending them for good.

This system worked well until. . . until *IT* happened.

Skylar and Fleur were out securing a potentially safe house to stay in for the night when a scent of decay and an eerie feeling filled the air. Skylar felt a cold shudder go up her spine. Even Fleur was on alert. His ears tensed and his haunch heightened on his back. A small growl escaped his mouth. One of those undead creatures was here. Shining her flashlight into the dark living room, that's when they saw it. Its eyes filled with immense hunger, focused on the pair. Its mouth snarling showing teeth that desired flesh. The undead being walked toward them with deadly intentions.

"Fleur", Skylar said to her trusted partner. "C'est le moment!"

Fleur had performed this maneuver many times. He would go around toward the creature drawing its attention while Skylar would attack from the other side. Fleur barked as he approached the decaying being and Skylar on cue trotted on the other side of the room to dispatch it. She knew they had only a few seconds so as not to attract others. She didn't notice the other undead being lying on the floor that grabbed her ankle. Skylar fell to the floor with a thud dropping her spear.

Fleur continued his barking drawing the decaying figure towards him while Skylar was fighting for her freedom to help her companion. Kicking her feet at the legless zombie on the floor, Skylar was within inches of grabbing her trusty spear. Fleur continued his noticeable barking and backed up into a corner. He waited for Skylar's command to attack unaware of her situation. Grasping the spear, Skylar swung it at the creature holding onto her ankle desiring the taste of her flesh. The tip of the spear managed to take half of the creature's face off, but not enough to stop.

Seeing Fleur's situation, Skylar yelled at him to attack. The courageous canine leaped into action and bit down on the walking zombie's left arm bringing it down to the ground. But the soulless being showed persistence in going after Fleur reaching for any part of him. Skylar swung the spear again cutting the legless creature's head open like a ripened watermelon. Freeing herself from its iron-like grasp, Skylar heard the most gut-wrenching sound ever.

"AAAARROOOOOO!!!!" howled Fleur as the vile being rolled over onto him. "NOOOO!" Skylar shrieked lifting herself on her feet. Fresh blood dripping from its mouth, the lifeless being looked at its next victim. Fleur, bleeding from the bite on his left front leg, started licking his wound as a natural reaction. With tears of extreme sadness and unfiltered rage, Skylar plunged her spear into the creature's skull. Pulling out the black blood-coated tip, she plunged it into its skull again. . . and again. . . and again cursing its existence.

Whimpering in pain, Skylar picked up the blood-soaked Fleur and embraced her injured companion. Tears poured from Skylar's eyes like a midsummer rainstorm. Her beautiful face twisted into a horrendous expression showing lament as her faithful partner took his last breath and crossed the rainbow bridge. Skylar found herself alone in a cruel dead world that stripped away hope of survival yet again.

Chapter 4: Melinda- Philadelphia

The City of Brotherly Love was nothing more than a silent graveyard, its streets eerily devoid of life. Sixteen-year-old Melinda crept through the rubble of her former high school, her breath shallow and quiet. The distant groans of the undead echoed off crumbling buildings, a constant reminder of the nightmare she was living.

She darted into an abandoned rowhouse and the stench of decaying, rotting flesh overwhelmed her senses. Melinda clutched the aluminum baseball bat she retrieved from a locker room at a high school, her only weapon, tighter. She had lost her family to the horde weeks ago, and now she was alone, surviving on sheer will and fleeting scraps of food.

"There's got to be some food here." thought Melinda. Her stomach grumbled noticeably as she sought out some sort of sustenance. Surviving two days without any food would make any hungry person seek anything to eat and Melinda hoped that this rowhouse would have something to silence her hunger pains. Cautiously she crept in through the living room, seeing the pictures of the family that once lived inside. Faded memories of a time much simpler, loving, and happier.

A sudden crash from the kitchen made her freeze. Heart pounding, she edged towards the noise. A figure stumbled into view, its rotting flesh hanging in tatters. Melinda swung the bat with all her might, the impact jarring her arms. The zombie fell, but more moans rose from the shadows.

Desperation fueled her as she fled up the stairs, the relentless undead hot on her heels. She barricaded herself in a bedroom and said a silent prayer, knowing the flimsy door wouldn't hold for long. Trapped and terrified, Melinda prepared to make her last stand in a city that had become her tomb. The once whole door had now been torn down with a ravenous horde coming into the bedroom intent on devouring her flesh.

THWACK! CRUNCH! SPLAT! Bodies of the undead piled on the floor of the bedroom as Melinda swung furiously knowing what her fate would be if she stopped. Hunger that triggered her survival mode eventually became rage. Rage for what happened to her family. THWACK! Rage for what happened to her city. CRUNCH! Rage for who she became. SPLAT!

After what seemed like an eternity, Melinda saw several of the undead lying at her feet. Crushed skulls, dislocated appendages, and blood black as midnight oozing out of their bodies were on display on the floor. Melinda then sat on the bed looking at what she had to do to survive. She had done this a couple of times, but this time was different. This deadly encounter was a major test, and she emerged victorious. Several minutes went by and Melinda calmed her fast-beating heart. It was at that moment that she quickly realized that both the living and the undead have something in common.

No matter if you're living or one of the undead, hunger will motivate you to seek food. Melinda recognized that she was now living in a world where she had to eat or be eaten. A living prey to an undead horde of predators whose numbers grew every day. Picking up her bat and standing up, Melinda made her way to the kitchen to find food. She'll need the energy to survive another night.

Chapter 5: Ava- San Diego

Ava sprinted through the deserted streets of San Diego, her heart pounding as the growls of the undead echoed behind her. Her younger siblings were trapped in their apartment, and she was their only hope for survival. The sixteen-year-old clutched the well-used baseball bat tightly, its bloodied edge a testament to her desperate struggle for living.

As she rounded the corner, the sight of her apartment complex filled her with a fleeting sense of hope. She dashed up the stairs, her breath ragged, and burst through the door. Her siblings' hopeful faces greeted her. The twins Nate and Jake, both 10 years old, and the youngest, Claire, age 7, were fortunate that Ava took care of them after their parents succumbed to the virus three weeks ago. It didn't just end their lives, but it ended their humanity as they became one of the undead.

As Ava began to settle in with her family, she heard something behind her. She looked and noticed the door of their second-floor apartment had been breached. The shambling figures had already broken in seeking their next meal.

Ava fought valiantly, her bat swinging with a ferocity born mixed with a sister's undying love and fear of losing everyone. But she was outnumbered. Teeth sank into her arm, and she let out a blood-curdling scream. An unbearable, searing pain coursing through her. As her vision blurred, she saw her siblings' horrified faces, and with her last breath, she whispered, "Run."

If only her siblings had listened.

Chapter 6: DeShaun- St. Louis

"Damn, I'm so hungry," thought 15-year-old DeShaun. It had been several grueling days since he had a bite to eat, and his hunger was unbearable. Having searched his neighborhood in his hometown, he found nothing edible. Yet he was determined to find something to satisfy his hunger.

Walking silently and avoiding unwanted attention, DeShaun ventured inside abandoned homes, churches, schools, and even a hospital to find any morsel of food. Each quest for food led to the same result. Nothing. He was growing more and more desperate with each passing step.

He tried his luck in the boarded-up supermarket that his family used to shop at hoping to find something. It had been two years since the outbreak happened and surely there'd be something that was still fresh to eat. Walking up and down the aisles, DeShaun found either bare shelves or items past their expiration date showing signs of mold and decay. He began moving toward the door when he heard something that caught his attention. Curiosity getting the better of him caused him to investigate. He didn't care if it was a wild animal like a cat or a dog or even a rat. He ate those before when food was extremely scarce and even though they didn't taste like his mother's cooking, they did satisfy his hunger and give him enough energy to press on.

The noise came from near the dairy section where spoiled milk and moldy cheese were displayed. Looking inside, he saw motion behind the items that had long been expired. DeShaun then decided to continue his investigation. "Please let it be something I can eat.", he hoped to himself. Opening the door to the back of the display and following where he saw the movement, he looked around to see what it was. Slowly he crept and ever vigilant, he continued his quest. It wasn't until he heard a loud gasp of air that he saw her.

"OH MY GOD!!! PLEASE NO!!!" the woman screamed at the morbid sight of DeShaun. His clothes tattered. His skin was pale. His body was nearly emaciated. His hunger led his feet toward the fearful woman. His grey, dead eyes focused on the prize. His decaying mouth opened ready to eat. He heard her scream, but her cries were met with unconcerned ears.

Her bloody screams were slowly silenced with the sounds of DeShaun growling, feasting on her flesh. "Mmmmm. . . delicious", DeShaun thought to himself as his hunger was being quenched. Being one of the undead isn't an ideal situation DeShaun wants to be in, but he must make the most of his newfound destiny.

Chapter 7: Luke- Atlanta

Luke crouched in the shadows of a crumbling Atlanta skyscraper, his breath shallow and quick. They were all over. The city had fallen silent, and its streets were now ruled by the undead. They were getting closer and closer to catching him. Every creak and rustle sent his heart racing, but he couldn't afford to stop. Their numbers increased every day. Survival was a constant game of cat and mouse, and the 13-year-old hated being the mouse.

Weeks had passed since the outbreak, and Luke found himself alone. His family was gone, taken by the virus and the chaos that followed. He remembered the looks and screams plaguing his dreams every night. He would often reminisce about the times before the virus hit. The sights of people out and about. The smell of the BBQ joint near his home. The hustling and bustling sounds of people on the crowded streets. Now, the only sounds he heard were the groans of the undead and the eerie, empty wind that whistled through the abandoned city. The smell was horrendous as the scent of rotting, dead flesh in the scorching Georgia summer heat filled the air. And of course, the sights of a once proud metropolitan area have now become an open-air tomb filled with despair.

As he silently crept through an alley, a sudden noise froze him. A shuffling figure emerged from the darkness. Its eyes lifeless and its mouth agape showing its teeth hungry for human flesh. Luke's grip tightened on the rusty crowbar he found on the street weeks ago. He knew he had to stay silent, unseen. Luke remembered the countless hours playing a video game where the main character was in a similar situation. Too much noise would give away his position.

Running at great lengths and extended time would only deplete his energy, and these zombies seem to have unlimited energy. Luke was trapped in this real-world deadly video game with no save points, no extra lives, and worst of all. . . no do-overs. One fatal mistake could be the difference between death and reaching the next level.

Holding his breath, he slipped past the zombie, despite his heart pounding. But he wasn't in the clear just yet. Another zombie was walking toward his direction; but with steadied breath and a tight grip on the crowbar, Luke hid inside a now abandoned gas station. Waiting for the undead figure to walk by, Luke took out a dimly lit flashlight to see if there were any flesh-eaters inside with him. Seeing none, he remembered the last video game he played. "Zombie Survivor" was a popular game for teens his age. While playing the game, Luke remembered that he had to cause distractions to lure the zombies to an area for his character's safety. But what could he find inside this gas station? Tires? Auto parts? Cars that were being worked on? Those would do him no good. He almost gave up hope until he saw some items that would be helpful and came up with a plan on how to use them.

Waiting for the street to clear, Luke ran back into the alley across from the gas station and remembered seeing a dumpster filled with trash and paper. Using his newly found items, a canister of gas, and 2 road flares he found at the gas station, he would set off a diversion tactic he perfected in his old video game. Emptying the canister into the dumpster, Luke devised an escape plan by hiding back in the gas station and playing the waiting game until every zombie in the area congregated around the fiery display that was sure to light up the ebony night sky. Luke then set off the road flares, careful to not get any unwanted attention. "Here goes nothing", Luke thought to himself and threw the flares into the gas-soaked dumpster.

FWOOSH!! The dumpster went ablaze as soon as the flares reached the inside of the dumpster. Luckily, Luke raced towards the gas station as soon as he saw the fire away from the glares of the undead roaming the streets. It wasn't that long for them to notice the amber flames shooting up in the sky. Slowly their curious nature got the best of them, thinking it was a sign of human flesh for them to feast and gathered in masses near the ongoing flames. Luke, lurking in the shadows of the abandoned gas station and ever observant, grabbed even more flares and some handheld tools that he figured would assist him in his quest to survive. After several minutes went by and carefully observing no signs of those undead beings walking the streets, Luke decided to leave.

The road to survival was narrow and fraught with danger, but Luke pressed on, determined to get to the next level and see another sunrise.

Chapter 8: Liang- Taiwan

Liang who fancied herself a resolute teenager, found herself racing through the abandoned streets of Taipei with her little brother Ming clinging to her side. The air was thick with the stench of death and decay, and the moans of the undead echoed around them.

The siblings had almost reached the safety of an old bunker when a horde of zombies emerged from the shadows. Liang shoved Ming inside and turned to face the creatures. She wielded a rusted metal pipe, determination in her eyes.

"Go, Ming! Don't look back!" she yelled.

Ming's terrified eyes met hers as he hesitated. "Liang!"

The zombies swarmed her, their cold hands grasping at her clothes, tearing at her flesh. She fought fiercely, her screams mingling with the growls of the undead.

With a final, desperate push, she managed to close the bunker door, sealing Ming inside unharmed.

As darkness closed in, her last thought was of Ming's safety, a bittersweet smile on her lips as the zombies claimed her.

Chapter 9: Trevor- Jamaica

Trevor sprinted through the chaotic streets of Kingston. The virus had just hit the Caribbean nations, and the millions of Jamaicans found themselves in the bullseye of the virus. His heart pounding in sync with the distant gunfire of the army and police shooting at the newly raised undead. The once vibrant town had become a desolate wasteland in a matter of a few days. Shadows of the undead lurk at every corner seeking fresh meat. His family's house was just a few blocks away, but each step felt like an eternity.

Suddenly, a blood-curdling scream echoed from a nearby alley. Trevor froze, his breath caught in his throat. He peered into the darkness, spotting a figure hunched over, gnawing on a lifeless body. The undead being's head snapped up, eyes locking onto him.

Panicking, Trevor raced down the road, the creature's guttural growls growing closer as it ran after him with a determined pace. He stumbled upon his house, the door ajar. Inside, the silence was deafening. He called out, his voice trembling, "Mama? Dada?"

A faint rustle came from the kitchen. He edged closer, gripping a kitchen knife. As he turned the corner, his blood ran cold. His mother, half-turned, reached out, with a ravenous hunger in her eyes.

His mother lurched at Trevor which caused her only son to cry out "Mama…NO!!!" But she was no longer his mother. She was a predator striking its prey. Trevor picked up the kitchen chair to keep his distance from his now-gone mother. With the knife in his hands, Trevor struck back, stabbing her once loving heart twice. Despite this, she persisted in her attack with what appeared to be uncontrollable rage. The metal chair continued to shield Trevor from his mother's attacks until one of the legs entered his mother's mouth and exited out the back of her skull. Her body went limp as Trevor pushed her onto the floor, the chair still impaled in her head.

Looking at the carnage he caused, a tear fell down Trevor's cheek. How can any son do this to their mother? That question will haunt his thoughts for the rest of his days not realizing that his actions saved his life. He then heard a familiar voice call out in the back.

"Son!" The raspy voice was barely audible, but Trevor recognized it. It was his father, Trevor Sr. Racing to the back bedroom his parents slept in with the knife in his hand, he saw his father with a bite mark around his collarbone near his neck. Blood was profusely pouring out from the makeshift gauze of the pillowcase that was from the bed.

"Dada! Whappen?!"

"Ya Mada . . . mi did get bit. Oh Lord!"

The pain on his father's face was beyond intense as the fresh bite not only drew crimson-colored blood from his neck but also caused his body's temperature to get hotter than a Caribbean sun in August. Trevor, dropping the knife by his side, did what he could to assist his father, but nothing could be done. He looked at his father one last time as his father closed his eyes entering the afterlife. Another tear ran down Trevor's face knowing that the recently turned 15-year-old was now all alone in a world going to Hell.

Trevor's mourning period for his parents was cut short. A short growl came from his father's mouth. His dark brown eyes were now replaced with dead gray pupils locking onto Trevor now sliding away from him. His father rolled over grabbing onto Trevor's left leg. Trevor frantically tried to kick away, but his father's strength seemed to be too much. Trevor then reached for the knife he stabbed his mother's undead body with and plunged it deep into his father's left eye. What was once his proud father now lying in a limp and lifeless shell for the second time. Trevor freed himself from his father's dead grasp visibly shaken. "Mi sorry Dada....mi sorry" was all Trevor could muster.

Being the top student at his school for winning several top awards in science in math, Trevor started to wonder. He quickly gathered his thoughts and assessed what happened. Both his mother and father had become one of those undead things that feasted on the living. His father had become one due to his mother's bite and both died again after something pierced their brains. Trevor then deduced that trying to kill these things as normal humans wouldn't work and that damaging their brains was the most effective way to keep these things dead. Trevor then gathered all the knives in the kitchen, his father's machete, and a hammer. He then left his parent's home which was now filled with death and ventured on to a new purpose. He would save as many people as possible and show them how to kill these undead creatures.

Resiliency runs deep in the blood of every Jamaican.

Chapter 10: Mindy- Oklahoma

Mindy's heart raced as she sprinted through the debris-strewn streets of Tulsa, Oklahoma. The proud, charming city was now a living nightmare. Sights of shattered windows, streets cluttered with abandoned cars, and remains of formerly living Oklahomans. The air hummed with an eerie silence, broken only by distant moans of the undead. Even the expected sunny skies took on a darker tone today. Much darker than usual.

With each step, fear gnawed at Mindy's resolve. The fifteen-year-old had lost her family weeks ago when the outbreak first hit. Now, survival was her only thought. But survival meant outrunning not just zombies, but the possible threat of Mother Nature and her fury around this time of the year.

Walking around in the safety of her new "home" within her father's gun shop, Mindy took stock of what she had scavenged from the nearby supermarket, noting which items she desperately needed. She also ensured that the windows and doors were locked and remained boarded up. In these times food, water, firearms, and ammo were worth more than silver and gold.

To say that Mindy was just a typical Southern girl would be an understatement. She was a perfect mixture of her mother, a former Miss Oklahoma beauty pageant contestant turned nurse, and her father, a former football standout at college turned local businessman who enjoyed the outdoors life. Mindy had been trained how to handle and use rifles and pistols since she was 7 and even went out on multiple deer hunts with her father. She even went out with him and her uncle on fishing trips as well. She knew how to survive in the wilderness and was determined to be a survivor in this zombie wilderness.

Mindy knew the supermarket nearby was completely emptied with mass hysteria sweeping the city. When the outbreak hit, people panicked as usual, hoarding all the food and supplies they could gather. Conditions grew even worse as people who once died from the outbreak were suddenly reanimated into walking corpses that devoured living people. That's how Mindy's parents succumbed to this madness.

They tried to help family members and close friends, until that one fateful day in which her uncle died from one of those walking corpse's bite. Her mother tended to his wounds while he displayed signs of extreme fever, fatigue, and sweating. After several minutes of painful agony, her uncle passed away. Her parents' home was filled with cries and hugs comforting each other after a tragic loss. It wasn't until a couple of minutes later that Mindy heard her mother cry as her once-dead uncle "woke up" from his deathly slumber and plunged his teeth into his sister-in-law's shoulder tearing a piece of flesh out and eating it. Blood flowed from the wound despite Mindy's mother trying her best to use towels as a tourniquet. Screams and chaos entered the house like an unwanted guest, and it made its presence well known. Her "uncle" started attacking everyone, biting and scratching anyone that came close. He was then joined by Mindy's mother who recently died from the fresh bite and blood loss. Mindy's father pulled out his .45, aiming at his now-deceased wife and brother, but couldn't find the courage to pull the trigger. Handing the pistol to Mindy, he handed her his car keys and ordered her to drive to the gun shop and lock it up.

The ghastly sight of her father being attacked by her mother was the last thing she witnessed before leaving. Reaching her father's gun shop and locking up the doors and windows, Mindy broke down crying hysterically knowing that for the first time in her life, she was all alone.

Despite this tragedy, Mindy showed immense survival skills and even realized that a shot to the head of the reanimated dead permanently stopped them. Gathering empty bags, as well as her father's .45 and extra loaded clips, Mindy ventured to another supermarket five miles away. Racing around the city silently to avoid unwanted attention, Mindy made her way to her destination. She had been here plenty of times after the outbreak and displayed signs that other survivors were here as well. With whatever limited supplies she could find, she loaded them into her bags and made her way to the secret entrance she made for herself. Once outside Mindy saw the telltale signs of what was coming. Dark skies. Ominous low-lying clouds forming a familiar shape. Loud roars echoing throughout the sky. Mindy knew when a tornado was coming, and she had to race back across the city to get to safety.

Running as fast as she could, she didn't care if she was followed by the dead roaming the streets. She figured that Mother Nature would blow away these zombies scattering them in the air like confetti. The clouds formed a funnel and Mindy figured that she had only a few precious minutes to run another mile and a half. But she wasn't the only one who noticed the storm. Those dreaded zombies knew the weather was changing quickly but didn't care. Satisfying their hunger was their primary concern. It was when Mindy was only less than a mile from her safehouse that she caught their attention, and they followed her. To say that several of those creatures followed her would be an understatement. It was as if she was being chased by an entire congregation of them with their numbers growing with each block Mindy races through.

Suddenly, the twister touched down ahead, its massive funnel tossing debris into the air. Mindy veered left, her legs burning with exertion. Behind her, she heard the guttural growls of approaching zombies. Panic surged as she realized she was trapped between two deadly forces of nature.

In a desperate dash, she escaped into her safehouse closing her makeshift door, praying the wooden boards and metal bars would shield her from both the undead and the wrath of the storm. The sounds of debris hitting the store and the zombies pounding walls and windows to feast on fresh flesh inside overwhelmed Mindy causing her to break down in a hysterical cry. Mother Nature dealt her a cruel hand in life, but she remembered what her parents always told her.

"We all want the sun and clear blue skies, but when storms come through, we still move on because as the Good Book teaches us, this too shall pass."

Mindy calmed herself down as the howling winds started shaking the building around. After a few minutes that seemed like an eternity, the skies cleared up. The sun started to shine again. Mindy climbed up on the roof of the gun shop and saw the remains of those zombies strewn all over the streets lifeless once again.

Taking in the scene, Mindy reminded herself, "This too shall pass."

Chapter 11: Brian- Minnesota

Brian's heart raced as he sprinted through the deserted, wintry streets of St. Paul, Minnesota. The once familiar snow-covered neighborhoods were now a labyrinth of danger and death. Behind him, groans grew louder, signaling the relentless pursuit of the undead.

Desperation guided Brian's feet to a neighborhood playground. With a gasp, he dove behind a pine tree, praying it would shield him from the horrors outside. The stench of decay mingled with fear as he pressed his trembling hands over his mouth, trying to quiet his ragged breaths. He had thought about the events that transpired to which he was a constant victim.

Two weeks ago, some mysterious illness spread throughout the different nations affecting millions, if not billions, of people. What was believed to be the common flu was far worse. People perished left and right. Survivors mourned their loss. While tears were shed and condolences were offered, the true illness took over. Those who recently passed away suddenly woke up with gray dead eyes and spoke in guttural moans. Loved ones at their side soon became victims of their attacks and eventual carriers of the illness.

Eighteen-year-old Brian found himself in a situation where he reacted to events that led him to being alone. His mother contacted the illness, and his father attempted to do what he could to assist her suffering. Try as his father could, the illness still won. Brian and his father found themselves unsure of the future without the matriarch of their family. Saying goodbye to his mother, Brian heard a sound coming from his mother that caused a nervous reaction to back away rapidly. His father leaned in to investigate and that's when Brian's life changed.

His mother's eyes opened sharply showing pale, gray pupils, a window to her lifeless being. Her mouth showing teeth like a snarling wolf about to attack. His puzzled father didn't react in time and his now-deceased mother plunged her teeth deep into her husband's neck. Brain, horrified at the morbid sight, backed against the wall, unsure of what to do except cry. After what seemed like an eternity and after his father lost an enormous amount of blood, his mother focused her attention on her frightened son. Brian's survival instincts kicked in and he escaped his parents' bedroom, grabbed his coat, and fled his childhood home entering an unknown world where survival is of great importance.

The minutes he spent reminiscing about how he became alone in a world where the dead came back to life stretched into an agonizing eternity. Shadows crept closer, accompanied by guttural snarls and scraping footsteps. Brian's heart threatened to burst from his chest as a pair of gray eyes scanned the darkness inches away. The undead shuffled past, its frigid breath chilling Brian to the core.

Frozen in terror, he waited until silence returned, dreading the moment he would have to flee once more into the nightmare that had consumed his world.

Chapter 12: Tawanna- Buffalo

High school sophomore Tawanna crouched on the top floor of McCarthy High School, heart racing, surrounded by the stench of decaying corpses that flooded outside. Buffalo's streets teemed with the undead, their hungry moans echoing through the frosty winter air. She clutched her baseball bat, slick with blood, hands trembling. Unsure of what's to come, especially with the sun setting earlier that day.

The day had started with her desperate scramble for safety as the outbreak engulfed the city. Countless people that once called the City of Good Neighbors home, now find themselves as either scattered survivors seeking something better, or one of the ravenous undead desperately seeking their next meal. Such was the case with Tawanna's mother a few days ago. The once proud nurse working at a local hospital was one of the first unfortunate souls to become one of the now walking corpses.

Days passed after her mother's change and the 15-year-old found herself alone for the first time in her young life. Her father, an Army captain, was called in for duty weeks before "The Outbreak" happened and the daily correspondence between him and his family trickled down to nothing. Once *it* happened, people found themselves unprepared and with more questions than answers and when she didn't hear from her mother, she presumed the worst.

She made the most of her newly found situation by staying indoors and remaining as quiet as possible. However, food was running low, and the frigid wintry conditions took away what little heat she had in her house. She did remember seeing shelter signs at her high school thinking it would be safe there. Having to break a window to her old homeroom on the first floor with her father's baseball bat, Tawanna made her way inside the high school. The furnace was still blowing hot air in the old brick building, and she figured that there was still some food to eat. Whatever food that wasn't eaten by the rats and other vermin was still edible for a month or two.

Tawanna feasted on cold peanut butter and jelly sandwiches, stale potato chips, and water from the water fountain in the school's cafeteria. All alone in a big school with those flesh-eating zombies outside in the blistering cold streets would be her second greatest fear. Little did she know that her first greatest fear was about to come true.

Having made her way to the foyer of her school, she heard what sounded like a helicopter flying overhead. Once she reached the foyer, she noticed that the front door was slightly open, and the floor was wet. Curiosity got the best of her to investigate the cause. Her feet cautiously approached the open door. Peering through the opening and seeing nothing outside in the gray sky-filled scenery. The sound of the helicopter sounded louder this time once she looked into the sky. Strange, she thought. Nothing was flown nor any cars or buses have been driven since The Outbreak occurred. It wasn't until she looked down and saw fresh footprints in the snow that her worst fear was confirmed. She wasn't alone in the school.

Closing the door ever so quietly and backing away ever so carefully, Tawanna looked around the open foyer for any signs of either the living. . . or one of the undead. Clutching the metal bat in her hand ever so tightly, she peered down the hallways and noticed a shadowy figure standing still, just observing her.

"Hey. . . you. . . you OK?", the words trying to find their way out of Tawanna's frightened mouth. Yet no verbal response was given. Only a guttural growl that grew louder with every step it took toward her. "Must be cold from being out there," Tawanna commented to the stranger. Still no response from the stranger. It wasn't until it approached closer that she found herself in her greatest fear.

Panic and fear struck her like a runaway train. Lighting in the hall flickered, revealing the grotesque form of the stranger inching closer toward her. Driven by its relentless hunger and guttural sounds, it was soon followed by several other strangers, intent on satisfying their hunger. Tawanna then raced up the stairs without hesitation until she reached the top floor. Believing to be safe and far away from those things, she slowed her breath and gathered her thoughts. Hearing more of those guttural sounds as well as the sounds of a low-flying helicopter, Tawanna peered from a window overlooking the entrance of the high school and saw more of those things entering inside. Her once steady heartbeat elevated once again as anxiety took over, especially with those things walking up the stairs after her.

Tawanna remembered going to the roof on a dare and instinctively raced there alerting several of the undead trapped on the top floor with her. Seeing the locked gate that led to the roof, Tawanna clutched her bat and raced her way toward it. She became a human juggernaut using her bat and speed to avoid being bitten only to stop and open the gate. Closing the gate and securing it, she then made her way outside atop the school. Taking a couple of deep breaths, Tawanna placed a couple of cinder blocks to keep the door closed and secured. Taking into her situation, she looked outside onto Main Street and saw a horde of those undead creatures walking aimlessly. It wasn't until she heard a low-flying helicopter that she looked up trying to get their attention.

Desperately seeking anything, she did manage to find a battery-operated lantern that still worked. Turning on her beacon of hope, she waved it around. She heard the door to the roof being banged as those undead beings made their way toward her and waved even faster, pleading for her rescue.

Circling around the school, the helicopter descended even lower above the roof. A man in a military-type uniform dropped down on a line and loudly asked "JUST YOU?" to which Tawanna replied "YES!" with tears coming down her eyes. Strapping her onto himself, the duo was raised into the helicopter. Embracing her rescuer tightly, a mixture of emotions flooded her eyes, and she began to cry. "Young lady are you ok?" she was asked to which she just shook her head up and down. "What's your name?" her rescuer asked. "Tawanna. . . Tawanna Jones" she replied during her cries.

After a few minutes, Tawanna settled down and noticed the uniform said U.S. Army on them. She then inquired "Do you know Captain Thomas Jones? He's my father."

Her rescuer shot her a puzzled and shocked look and then yelled to the pilots in the cockpit, "Hey Cap, you ain't gonna believe this."

Printed in Dunstable, United Kingdom